LEGENDARY CREATURES

Mythical Beasts and Spirits from Around the World

ADAM AUERBACH

Christy Ottaviano Books

Little, Brown and Company
New York Boston

NORTH
AMERICA

Thunderbirds

Mishipeshu

Cipactli

Merfolk

SOUTH
AMERICA

Alicanto

Fenrir

EUROPE

Dragons

Golem

Unicorns

Chimera

Phoenix

Triton

Griffins

Ziz

Scorpion
people

Apep

Bennu

Rocs

Mami
Wata

Simurg

AFRICA

Miengu

Khodumodumo

N

W

E

S

ASIA

Qilin →

Navagunjara

← Dragons →

Bulgae

Baku

Ningyo

Yawkyawks

Mimi

AUSTRALIA AND OCEANIA

Te Ika-a-Māui

CONTENTS

AUTHOR'S NOTE

MYTHS AND FOLKTALES are stories of our dreams, fears, and aspirations. Some have been passed on for generations through oral tradition. Others were written down long ago. Many myths were meant to answer questions about our world: How was the universe created, and did anything exist before that? What causes day and night? The explanations often take fantastical form.

This collection is a celebration of some of the wondrous beings in world mythology and folklore. It is a book of legendary creatures—powerful spirits, ancient gods, fierce monsters, and helpful beasts.

The creatures in this collection come from all over the world. While there are stories of countless mythical beings, this sampling was chosen to show a variety of creatures with unique qualities. If any of these creatures capture your imagination, I hope you will seek out more information on them, especially from the parts of the world where they originated. I find each of these creatures magnificent in their own way, and I hope you enjoy learning about them.

ALICANTO

Place of Origin: Chile

THE BIRD WITH GOLDEN FEATHERS

If you see something shining in the night of the Atacama Desert, it may be a distant campfire or a traveler's lantern. Then again, it just might be an Alicanto. The Alicanto is a magnificent bird with gold or silver feathers. Its eyes glow with a strange light, and its body gleams against the shadowy landscape.

A DIET OF PRECIOUS METAL

The Alicanto's metallic sheen comes from its food; it loves to eat gold and silver ore. The coloring of its feathers depends upon which of the two precious metals it has been eating. Due to its diet, the Alicanto is too heavy to fly. Instead, it runs across the ground with its wings spread. When the Alicanto is particularly well-fed it can barely crawl.

GREAT REWARD AND GREAT PERIL

Those who witness the Alicanto may be tempted to follow it because it can lead the lucky to caves full of gold or silver. Though it may bring good fortune, people who trail this bird should be careful. If the Alicanto sees its pursuers, it may lead them off a cliff. It might also turn off its glow, leaving the unlucky stranded in complete darkness.

APEP

Place of Origin: Egypt

SERPENT OF CHAOS

When the gods of ancient Egypt created the universe, the great serpent Apep became angered. He wanted reality to remain chaotic, without any shape. In the time before creation, there was no up or down, no sky or earth. Everything had been formless, and Apep was determined to make it so again.

ENEMY OF THE SUN

Enraged by the creation of the world, Apep lay in wait ready to destroy it. When the sun god Ra sailed by on his ship, the serpent opened its jaws to swallow him and plunge the world into darkness.

A NEW DAY DAWNS

The gods had to meet Apep in battle. With the help of mortals' prayers, they were able to slay Apep and save Ra. The sun rose for a new day, but so did Apep. Each evening, Apep tried to swallow Ra in an endless cycle. Thankfully, the gods aided by prayer always prevailed, and the sun could rise in the morning.

Baku

Place of Origin: Japan

Nightmare Eater

The Baku is a helpful creature that feeds on dreams. If you are troubled by nightmares, you need only repeat three times, "Baku, please come and eat my dream." The Baku will gladly gobble up your nightmare.

Patchwork Creature

The gods created the Baku from the leftover parts of other animals. It has an elephant's trunk and tusks, a tiger's claws, a rhino's eyes, and an ox's tail.

A Word of Warning

It might seem like a good idea to call the Baku at night, but be careful! The Baku is a very hungry beast. If you call on it too much, it will eat your good dreams as well as your nightmares.

BULGAE

Place of Origin: Korea

Dogs from the Land with No Light

There is a world of darkness called Gamangnara. Long ago, the king of Gamangnara wished to steal the light of our world, so he sent fiery dogs to capture the sun and moon. These dogs from the dark kingdom are called Bulgae.

Stealing the Sun and Moon

When the first Bulgae bit the sun, the sun was too hot for the dog to hold in its mouth. The Bulgae ran back to the world of darkness, without anything to show for itself. When the second Bulgae bit the moon, the moon was too cold, and the dog had to let it go. This Bulgae, too, returned to Gamangnara with nothing.

Creators of Eclipses

To this day, the king of Gamangnara longs for our sun and moon. The Bulgae are still trying to bring them back for their master. Whenever there is an eclipse, and part of the sun or moon is covered in shadow, the Bulgae are said to have caused it. Fortunately, the Bulgae remain unable to complete their task, and the sun and moon always return to normal.

CHIMERA

Place of Origin: Ancient Greece

THREE-HEADED THREAT

The monstrous Chimera had three different heads—a lion, a goat, and a serpent. The Chimera terrorized the land, and because of her fiery breath, no one dared to stop her.

BATTLE IN FLIGHT

The fire-breathing Chimera was finally defeated with the help of Pegasus, a winged horse. A warrior named Bellerophon rode Pegasus, flying high in the air, where the Chimera could not reach him. Bellerophon was able to slay the beast by tying a block of lead to his spear. The Chimera's flame melted the lead, which dripped into the monster's mouth, quenching her flame forever.

HER NAME LIVES ON

The Chimera's name is often associated with any creature made from parts of different animals.

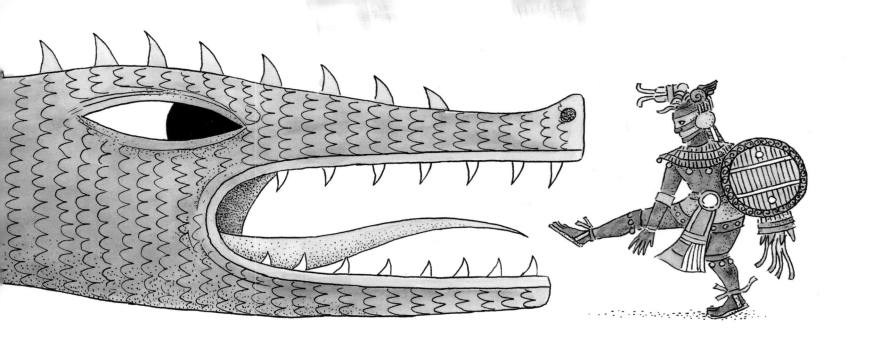

CIPACTLI

Place of Origin: Mexico

A WORLD COVERED IN WATER

When the Aztec gods created the world, it was only water. Swimming through the endless sea was the enormous Cipactli. It resembled a giant crocodile. Cipactli was always hungry—it had a mouth full of sharp teeth at every joint of its body.

THE GODS STEP IN

The gods soon realized that the ever-hungry Cipactli would devour anything they created. A god named Tezcatlipoca lured the ravenous beast with his foot. The gods defeated the distracted Cipactli, but not before Tezcatlipoca's foot was eaten.

THE CREATION OF OUR WORLD

After Cipactli's demise, the gods used its body to create the heavens, the underworld, and the earth with humans to populate the land. The creature that threatened to consume all life wound up becoming the home that nurtures it.

DRAGONS

Place of Origin: Worldwide

AWE-INSPIRING BEASTS

The dragon is one of the most amazing and recognizable of all mythic creatures. Dragons take many forms but often share some traits, such as scales or serpentlike bodies. Many have horns and sharp claws. Some dragons are wise and helpful, while others are dangerous and greedy.

DRAGONS OF EUROPE

The dreaded European dragons are reptilian. They can be snakelike serpents or walk on four legs. Sometimes they have wings and occasionally multiple heads. They often breathe fire or deadly poison. Many dragons of Europe can be found guarding treasure. They devour livestock and even people. Great warriors of ancient Greece and knights from medieval times have clashed with these fearsome beasts. Saint Martha of Bethany was said to have subdued a dragon by showing it a cross, sprinkling it with holy water, and tying it up with her girdle.

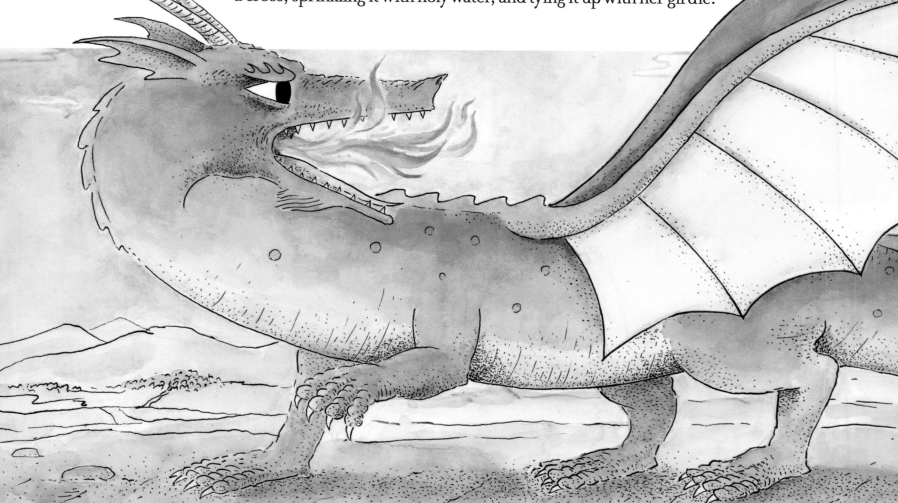

DRAGONS OF EAST ASIA

Dragons of China are long and serpentine. They have the horns of a stag, head of a camel, eyes of a demon, ears of a cow, and the neck of a snake. Their belly is that of a clam, and their scales are that of a carp. They have the claws of an eagle, and the soles of their feet belong to a tiger. They are usually wingless, but are able to fly nonetheless. Many dragons carry a pearl—these glowing stones are symbols of power. Four dragon kings rule over the seas, and there are dragons in lakes and rivers all across China.

These powerful creatures traveled far, and variations inhabit waters all over East Asia. When spring arrives, they head to the skies to create clouds and bring helpful rain. They may appear or disappear at will and can take on the forms of other animals, including people.

DRAGONS EVERYWHERE

There are dragons or dragonlike beings all over the world. Many cultures tell stories of powerful and scaly beasts. Few creatures capture our imaginations as much as dragons.

FENRIR

Place of Origin: Scandinavia

THE BIGGEST WOLF

Fenrir was no ordinary wolf. His parents were Loki, the most mischievous Norse god, and the giantess Angrboda. When the other gods saw Fenrir, they knew he was trouble, so they decided to keep an eye on him. Everyone soon noticed that Fenrir was growing much larger than expected. The beast had become a giant, and he would only get bigger. Something had to be done.

A PLAN IS FORMED

The gods approached Fenrir with strong shackles. Fenrir knew he could easily break the chains but allowed the gods to put them on him so that he could show off his strength. After Fenrir broke free, the gods brought him even stronger shackles. Fenrir quickly broke them as well.

CAPTURED BY ENCHANTMENT

The gods then brought Fenrir a thin ribbon and asked whether he could break free from it, too. Although it looked fragile, the ribbon was magical and far stronger than the heavy shackles. Fenrir suspected that he was being tricked. As a sign of good faith, a brave god named Tyr put his hand in Fenrir's jaws while the other gods tied the wolf up with the magical ribbon. When Fenrir realized he could not escape the ribbon, he chomped down. Poor Tyr lost a hand, but he had saved the day. Fenrir was captured and for a time the gods were no longer threatened. It was foretold that Fenrir would one day escape and help bring about the end of their reign.

GOLEM

Place of Origin: Central Europe

MAN OF CLAY

Long ago, in Prague, a rabbi made a very special sculpture. He molded clay from the riverside into the shape of a man. With holy magic, he brought his sculpture to life. The living clay man was called the Golem.

PROTECTOR OF THE JEWISH PEOPLE

The Golem was made to protect the Jewish people of Prague from those who refused to let them live peacefully. Each night he patrolled the streets, keeping his people safe from harm. The Golem was very strong and had the power to become invisible. He also helped around the neighborhood, lifting heavy objects for others and doing chores.

GOLEM ON THE LOOSE

No one knows exactly why, but one day the Golem became destructive. Some say that he was made to work on the Sabbath, a day of rest. Others claim that the Golem fell in love with someone who did not love him back, causing him to become deeply troubled. Whatever the reason, the Golem was now a danger to the people he was created to protect. The rabbi had to return the Golem's life force to the heavens. No longer alive, the Golem again became a simple clay sculpture. Some whisper that he is still hidden in Prague, waiting to be brought back to life should his people need him.

GRIFFIN

Place of Origin: Middle East

MAJESTIC BEASTS

The griffin has the body of a lion and is said to be eight times as strong. Its head and wings are an eagle's, but the creature is a hundred times mightier. A griffin's front legs can resemble those of either animal. These creatures were first seen in North Africa and the Middle East. They migrated to ancient Greece and then to the rest of Europe.

FEARSOME GUARDIANS

In ancient times, it was thought that gold nuggets could be found in the underground nests of griffins. Those who tried to steal a griffin's treasure put themselves at great risk; they found the beasts ready to guard their eggs and gold with sharp claws.

SYMBOLS OF POWER AND NOBILITY

In medieval times, griffins were regarded as noble creatures. Their feathers were said to cure blindness, and it was thought that their claws could detect poison. Knights and nobles put pictures of griffins on their banners and shields. These images were meant to show majesty, as well as fierce power in battle.

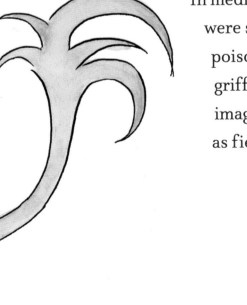

TE IKA-a-MĀUI

Place of Origin: Polynesia

MĀUI

Māui was a great hero of the Māori people. When Māui was born he seemed lifeless. His mother wrapped him in strands of her hair and threw him into the ocean, where spirits cared for him. Māui returned to land very much alive—he was a powerful young trickster, and he soon rejoined his human family.

THE BIGGEST CATCH EVER MADE

One day Māui went fishing with his brothers. He brought his magic hook, which was made from one of his ancestor's bones. For bait, he used a tiny bit of his own blood. He lowered his fishing line deeper than he ever had before.

Māui's brothers did not think he would catch a thing, but they were wrong. Something began to tug on the line, and it felt quite large. Māui called for his brothers to help haul his catch to the surface. It was a fish so enormous that it seemed to fill the sea.

THE NORTH ISLAND OF NEW ZEALAND

Impatient, Māui's brothers jumped on the fish and immediately began to carve it up for food, creating a landmass with many peaks and valleys. The incredible fish was so huge that its floating body became an island named Te Ika-a-Māui, the fish of Māui. It is also known as the North Island of New Zealand.

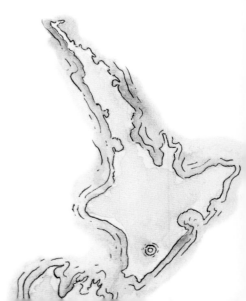

KHODUMODUMO

Place of Origin: Lesotho, South Africa

SWALLOWING MONSTER

Long ago, there lived an ever-hungry monster called Khodumodumo. He consumed any living thing he found, and nothing could escape him. Khodumodumo gulped up gentle animals, fearsome beasts, and even people. Soon it seemed that every creature that lived had been eaten.

A HERO IS BORN

One woman, who was about to have a baby, managed to save herself from Khodumodumo. She covered her body in ashes and buried herself in dung, and the monster passed by without seeing her. After Khodumodumo was gone, she gave birth. As soon as the infant touched the ground, he was fully grown. It was clear to the woman that her son, whom she named Ditaolane, was wise and would be a great warrior.

LIFE RETURNS TO THE WORLD

Ditaolane asked his mother why the two of them were alone on earth. She told him of the terrible Khodumodumo, and Ditaolane immediately went off to face the monster. He found Khodumodumo resting after having gorged himself. The hero and the demon fought, and Ditaolane was the victor. He sliced Khodumodumo open, and all the creatures who had been eaten climbed out alive. The world was full of life again, and Ditaolane became known as a great hero and leader.

MERFOLK

Place of Origin: Worldwide

PEOPLE OF THE SEA

Merfolk, beings with the top half of a person and the bottom half of a fish, swim in waters around the world. Some are gods or powerful spirits, while others are mortal creatures. They are as mysterious as the oceans and can be both helpful and dangerous.

POWERFUL DEITIES AND WATER SPIRITS

In many parts of western, central, and southern Africa, the most powerful water spirit is called Mami Wata. She can appear as a mermaid or be completely human in shape. She has the power to heal the sick and bring good fortune but can also drown those who anger her. Water spirits in Cameroon are known as Miengu (Jengu for just one). They can bring messages to and from the spirit world.

Triton, a merman from ancient Greece, was the son of Poseidon, god of the sea. He lived with his parents in a golden underwater palace and blew a twisted shell to calm or raise the waves. The Greeks and Romans called all mermen Tritons.

Yawkyawks are water spirits of Australia and can bring helpful rain. They live in water holes and often resemble mermaids, with hair made of strands of algae. Some say they can transform into dragonflies or grow legs at night to travel across land.

Ningyos of Japan are human-fish hybrids, with the head of a person and sometimes arms that end in webbed fingers. They are often monstrous in appearance. Eating a Ningyo can grant long life. Nevertheless, those hoping to fish for one of these creatures should think twice—catching a Ningyo can bring misfortune and dangerous storms.

SAILORS' TALES

Sailors around the world have long told of beings with fish tails in place of legs. The sighting of one of these merfolk could foretell a tempest. On the other hand, there are stories of sailors falling in love with these fish-tailed beings. Either way, witnessing a mermaid is not to be taken lightly.

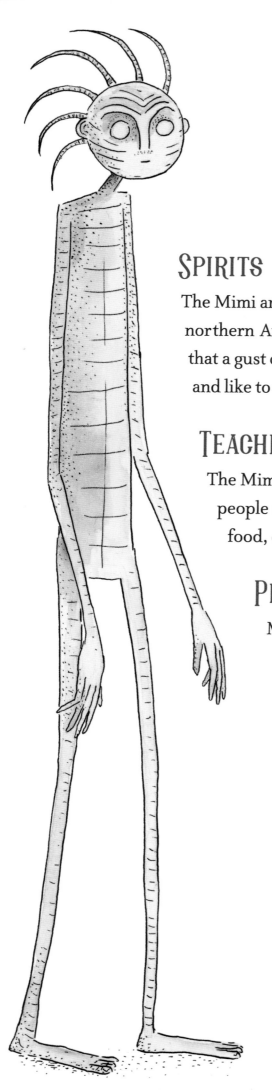

Mimi

Place of Origin: Northern Australia

Spirits Between the Rocks

The Mimi are nature spirits who live in the rock crevices of Arnhem Land in northern Australia. Their bodies and limbs are long and thin like twigs—so thin that a gust of wind might snap them in two. They only come out in calm weather and like to eat yams.

Teachers from the Past

The Mimi lived in Australia long before humans. When the first Aboriginal people arrived, the Mimi taught them important skills, such as hunting for food, cooking, and painting. These days Mimi are seldom seen.

Protectors of the Animals

Mimi take care of the animals in Arnhem Land. They consider the wallabies and other creatures of the wilderness to be their pets. Although Mimi were helpful to people in the past, they may seek to punish humans who do not respect the wildlife around their rocky homes.

MISHIPESHU

Place of Origin: North America's Great Lakes

THE GREAT LYNX

Mishipeshu, whose name means the Great Lynx, stalks the watery depths of North America's Great Lakes, home of the Anishinabe peoples. Mishipeshu resembles a panther covered in scales, with horns crowning its head. Sharp spikes run down Mishipeshu's back, all the way to the end of its serpentine tail.

LORD OF THE DEEP

Mishipeshu has power over the creatures that swim in the deep. Those traveling across the Great Lakes should be wary and pay their respects to this underwater panther. It can create storms and

whirlpools with its tail and sink a boat that enters its territory. Mishipeshu guards copper mines and will attack any being who tries to steal the metal from its home. It has been said that Mishipeshu's horns are made of copper.

THUNDERBIRDS

Mishipeshu is a master of the world below the surface, and it has a counterpart in the skies above. The Animikii, often called Thunderbirds, are powerful beings of the air. They protect humanity and can create thunder with the flapping of their wings, hurling lightning at the creatures of the underworld.

Navagunjara

Place of Origin: India

Wondrous Beast

The Navagunjara is made up of parts from nine different creatures. It has the head of a rooster, the neck of a peacock, the waist of a lion, and the hump of a bull. Its tail is a snake. The Navagunjara has one human arm and stands on three legs: an elephant's, a tiger's, and an antelope's.

Friend or Foe?

One day a mighty warrior named Arjuna came across the Navagunjara. He had never seen a creature so odd looking and thought it could be dangerous. Arjuna drew his bow and arrow. Then he noticed that the animal was delicately holding a lotus flower and realized it was peaceful. Arjuna decided not to harm the Navagunjara.

A Hero's Test

The Navagunjara was actually Krishna, a god of compassion and love. Krishna had taken the shape of the Navagunjara so that he could test Arjuna. The god wanted Arjuna to prove that he was wise enough to respect all things, even something as strange as the Navagunjara.

PHOENIX

Places of Origin: Egypt, Ancient Greece

ANCIENT BIRD

The Phoenix is a brilliantly colored and truly unique bird—there is only one in the world. It lives for five hundred years, then it takes flight. Some claim that it flies from the Arabian Peninsula to Egypt, but its final destination is a mystery.

REBORN IN FIRE

When the Phoenix reaches the end of its flight, it makes a nest of twigs and spices and sets it aflame. The Phoenix lets itself be consumed by the fire, but that is not the end of its story. From the flames, a new Phoenix majestically emerges. The new Phoenix will do the same when it becomes five hundred years old, creating an endless cycle of rebirth. This cycle is seen as a symbol of renewal, immortality, and the sun.

BENNU

The Bennu bird of ancient Egypt may have been the very first Phoenix. It resembled a large heron, and like the sun, it was able to continually renew its life. This ancient bird was said to have created itself and then played a role in the creation of the world. It stood on the newly formed ground that rose from the waters. When the Bennu called out, the world began.

Roc

Place of Origin: Middle East

Giant of the Skies

The roc is a bird so enormous that it is capable of carrying off an elephant for its meal. It resembles a massive eagle, and the beating of its wings can create winds of terrific force.

Sinbad and the Roc's Egg

Sinbad was a sailor who encountered many wonders and perils during his voyages. Once, he and his crew spied a giant egg on the shore of an island. Sinbad realized that the egg belonged to a roc, but his crew foolishly chose to eat it. Sinbad quickly set sail from the island, though it was too late. The enraged adult rocs appeared in the sky. The furious birds hurled boulders and destroyed Sinbad's ship. Sinbad barely managed to escape.

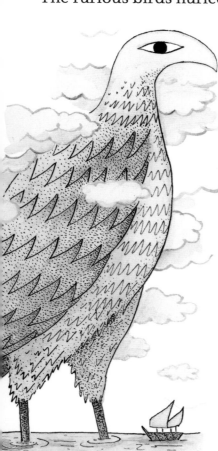

Ziz and Simurgh

There are more giant birds in the Middle East. Jewish mythology tells of the Ziz. It rules over other birds, and its wings are large enough to block out the sun. If the feet of the Ziz rest on the seafloor, its head can touch the sky.

The Simurgh of Iran is an enormous peacock, with the head of a dog and claws of a lion. Like the roc, it can prey on elephants. Some have even seen whales in its claws.

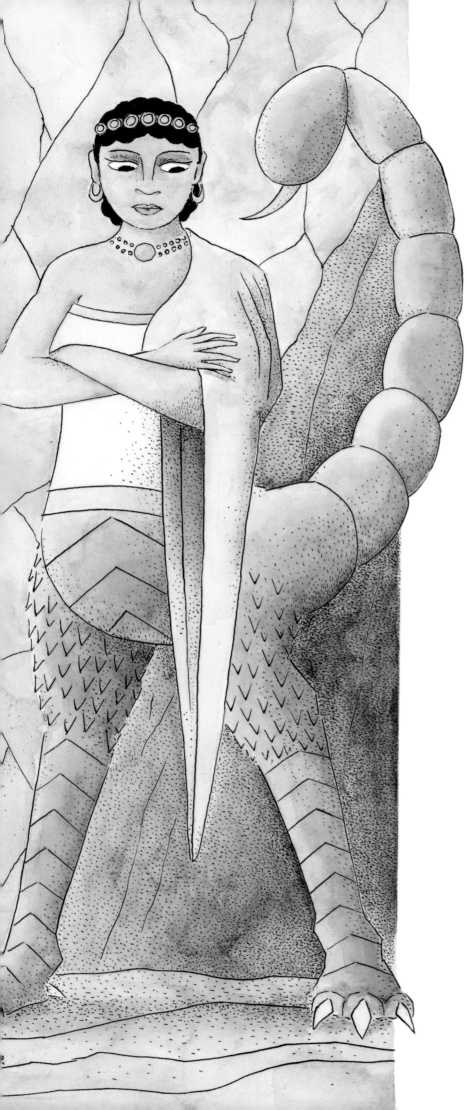

SCORPION PEOPLE

Place of Origin: Middle East

IMPOSING GIANTS

The Girtablilu, known as scorpion people, are towering giants. Their top halves appear human, but their bottom halves end in scorpion tails. Their feet resemble the sharp claws of birds of prey. Scorpion people are tall enough to touch the sky and can bring instant doom with a single gaze.

SOLDIERS AND GUARDIANS

In the early days of the world, there was a war among the gods. Tiamat, an ancient goddess of the sea, was fighting younger gods for control of the universe. She created the scorpion people to serve as soldiers in her army. The newer gods eventually defeated Tiamat and her forces, but the scorpion people remained.

After the war of the gods, some scorpion people became guards at the mountains of Mashu. Each day they open the gates to let the sun god Shamash pass out of the world of darkness. They reopen the gates on Shamash's return at day's end.

GILGAMESH

There was once a powerful king named Gilgamesh, whose mother was a god. He was mortal but wished to live forever, so he set out on a journey beyond the mountains of Mashu to seek the advice of Utnapishtim, the world's only immortal man. At the gates of Mashu, he met two scorpion people. Even the mighty Gilgamesh feared these giants. At first the scorpion people would not let Gilgamesh move forward, but eventually they took pity on him and allowed him to pass through the mountain to the land beyond.

Gilgamesh learned from Utnapishtim that he could not live forever unless the gods themselves chose to grant his wish. Unfortunately for him, they did not. Gilgamesh would one day be gone from the world, but his adventures, including his encounter with the scorpion people, would live on.

UNICORNS

Places of Origin: Europe, East Asia

Magnificent Horns

The unicorn is a magical horse with a single horn on its forehead. These radiant beasts live all across Europe. They are gentle creatures of the wild and are kind to their fellow animals. Unicorn horns possess healing properties, and these creatures have been known to dip their horns into poisoned lakes, purifying the waters for other animals.

Hunted Across Europe

Long ago, unicorns were hunted for the magical healing power of their horns, as well as their beauty. Luckily, they were usually swift enough to avoid capture. Those who believed they owned unicorn

horns had often been duped and purchased rhinoceros or narwhal horns instead. The narwhal is a type of whale with a single horn. Its horn is actually a giant tooth. Narwhal horns are beautiful, but unlike unicorn horns, they are not magical.

Qilin

The Qilin of China is another magical creature that can possess a single horn. Its body is shaped like a horse or deer, covered in scales. The Qilin's dragonlike head often has a single stag's horn in the center and can sometimes have two.

The Qilin may appear fearsome, though it is only dangerous to the wicked. This benevolent creature protects the virtuous and brings good luck. It is so gentle that it will not walk upon grass for fear of harming the plants. Versions of the Qilin are found across East Asia.

Creature Notes for the Curious

 In 1832, prospector Juan Godoy found a large outcrop of silver in the Atacama Desert, sparking the Chilean silver rush. According to legend, an **Alicanto** led him to the precious metal. The famous Argentine writer Jorge Luis Borges introduced the Alicanto worldwide when he included the creature in his *Book of Imaginary Beings*. He credited Chilean folklorist Julio Vicuña Cifuentes for his account of the bird.

 **Apep** is also referred to as Aapep, Apepi, Apophis, or Apopis. He appears in numerous ancient Egyptian artworks and texts. *The Book of Overthrowing Apep*, part of a papyrus from 305 BCE in the British Museum, describes prayers to protect the sun god Ra against the serpent of chaos.

 The Japanese **Baku** evolved from the Chinese creature Mo, which does not possess dream-eating abilities (although does provide protection from sickness and misfortune). The Baku has been depicted in many artworks, including an illustration by Japanese artist Katsushika Hokusai. The Baku has been said to have the tail of an ox. It has also been rendered with a bushy tail similar to that of a Karashishi, a type of mythical guardian creature. In this book the Baku is illustrated with a Karashishi-like tail.

 The **Bulgae**, which translates to "fire dogs" in English, come from a Korean folktale. In Chinese folklore, a different dog, Tiangou, resides in the heavens and eats the moon.

 The story of Bellerophon and the **Chimera** can be found in the *Iliad*, an epic tale by the ancient Greek poet Homer. It is also recounted in the Library of Apollodorus, which centuries later compiled Greek myths and legends. The Chimera was said to terrorize the land of Lycia, which was located in what is now Turkey, but the myth itself comes from Greece.

 The gods' battle with **Cipactli** is one of several Aztec creation myths. The story of Cipactli itself varies. Sometimes it is the goddess Tlaltecuhtli who takes the form of the monster with mouths at every joint and whose body forms the world. The first section of the Aztec calendar belongs to Cipactli (a caiman or crocodile).

 There are many stories of European **dragons** and dragon slayers. *The Golden Legend*, a medieval book recounting the lives of saints, tells of Saint Martha defeating the dragon.

 Second-century scholar Wang Fu described the parts of a Chinese dragon during the Han dynasty. The creature was a symbol of the Chinese emperor, and relief sculptures of nine dragons decorate three tiled walls in China. Scholars believe the Chinese dragon spread throughout East Asia and took on different characteristics in each culture.

 Snorri Sturluson's *Prose Edda*, a thirteenth-century Icelandic collection of Norse mythology, tells the story of **Fenrir**. During Ragnarok, the destruction of the gods, Fenrir will break free and swallow Odin, the All-father, first among the gods. Vidar, a son of Odin, will then avenge his father and slay Fenrir.

 The term *golem*, meaning a shapeless mass, dates back to the Hebrew Bible; in the Middle Ages it came to mean a body brought to life. In many versions of the tale of the **Golem**, the rabbi was Judah Loew ben Bezalel, who lived in sixteenth-century Prague. The Golem was activated in various ways, including by writing the Hebrew letters for truth on its forehead or placing the written name of God in its mouth.

 **Griffins** appear in the artwork of Mesopotamia and Egypt as early as 3300 BCE. From there, they spread to ancient Greece. In the fifth century BCE, the Greek historian Herodotus described griffins as guardians of gold in the north of Europe. In medieval Europe, griffins were seen as a symbol of goodness, and sculptures of the creatures were sometimes put in churches.

New Zealand adopted **Te Ika-a-Māui** as an official name of its North Island, in 2013. The tale of **Māui** catching the giant fish is Māori, but the legendary trickster appears in oral traditions all across Polynesia. He was said to be responsible for creating the Hawaiian Islands, which were parts of the ocean floor he and his brothers pulled up with his hook.

The story of Ditaolane and **Khodumodumo**, also called Kammapa, comes from the oral tradition of the Basotho people of southern Africa. After he slayed the monster Khodumodumo, Ditaolane's people turned against him out of fear and jealousy. Nevertheless, when he died, his heart flew to the sky, where he continued to watch over them.

Different varieties of **merfolk** exist all over the world. **Miengu** are one of several types of African water spirits that resemble mermaids. Long ago, some African water spirits resembled merfolk and others took different forms, such as snakes and crocodiles. As time went by, many more spirits changed to become merfolk. In artworks, **Mami Wata** is often shown holding a snake. **Triton** has been depicted in artwork wrestling with the mighty warrior Hercules. **Yawkyawks** appear in Australian Aboriginal artworks and oral traditions. They are said to occasionally marry humans but may return to life in the water. Japanese artist Toriyama Sekien included the **Ningyo** in one of his eighteenth-century collections of ghosts and monsters. Carved images of European mermaids were sometimes used as figureheads for sailing ships. They appear in many works of art and folktales across the continent.

Mimi spirits come from the Australian Aboriginal oral tradition and appear in rock paintings in Arnhem Land. Some stories present Mimi as helpful, and some show them as untrustworthy, even dangerous. They have occasionally been described as having a taste for eating people but usually prefer yams.

To avoid the wrath of **Mishipeshu**, travelers crossing its watery territory would sometimes offer it tobacco. The Great Lynx is depicted in a rock painting in Lake Superior Provincial Park, Ontario, Canada, which is attributed to the Ojibwa people. Anishinabe **Thunderbirds** appear in many artworks, including rock paintings and decorations for bags or pouches. Different versions of Thunderbirds appear in the traditions of many Indigenous peoples of North America.

The story of Arjuna and the **Navagunjara** appears in the Hindu epic *Mahabharata*, in the version written by fifteenth-century Odia poet Sarala Das. Many paintings of the Navagunjara originated in Odisha, India.

The ancient Greek historian Herodotus learned of the **Bennu** bird on a visit to Egypt. He called the bird **Phoenix** and said it appeared in the Temple of the Sun every five hundred years. Centuries later, the Roman poet Ovid described Phoenix's fiery rebirth in *Metamorphoses*.

The story of Sinbad and the **roc**'s egg is included in *The Thousand and One Nights*, a collection of Arabic folktales. The **Ziz** is described in the Talmud and briefly mentioned in the Hebrew Bible. The **Simurgh** has been depicted with a bird's body and a dog's head, and also as a completely birdlike creature of enormous size. It appears in the Persian epic *Shāh-nāmeh* by Ferdowsī and in many Iranian artworks.

The sea goddess Tiamat's creation of the **scorpion people** is recounted in *Enuma elish*, the Mesopotamian creation epic. Another Mesopotamian text, the *Epic of Gilgamesh*, tells the story of Gilgamesh and the scorpion people.

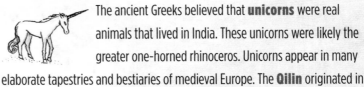

The ancient Greeks believed that **unicorns** were real animals that lived in India. These unicorns were likely the greater one-horned rhinoceros. Unicorns appear in many elaborate tapestries and bestiaries of medieval Europe. The **Qilin** originated in China and has variations throughout East and Southeast Asia. A Qilin was said to have appeared before the pregnant mother of Chinese philosopher Confucius. Its appearance foretold a great future for her child.

SOURCES

American Natural History Museum. www.amnh.org.

Berndt, Ronald M., and Catherine H. Berndt. *The Speaking Land: Myth and Story in Aboriginal Australia*. Rochester, VT: Inner Traditions International, 1994.

Gardner, John, and John Maier, trans. *Gilgamesh*. New York: Knopf, 1984.

Homer. *The Iliad*. Translated by Robert Fagles. New York: Penguin, 1990.

Kendall, Laurel, Mark A. Norell, and Richard Ellis. *Mythic Creatures and the Impossibly Real Animals Who Inspired Them*. Adapted from the American Museum of Natural History exhibition *Mythic Creatures: Dragons, Unicorns & Mermaids*. New York: Sterling Signature, 2016.

Lyons, Malcolm C., trans. *The Arabian Nights: Tales of 1001 Nights*. Vol. 2. New York: Penguin, 2008.

McLeish, Kenneth. *Myth: Myths and Legends of the World Explored*. New York: Facts on File, 1996.

Metropolitan Museum of Art. www.metmuseum.org.

National Folk Museum of Korea. *Encyclopedia of Korean Folk Culture*. folkency.nfm.go.kr/en/main.

Okada, Barbra Teri. *Netsuke: Masterpieces from the Metropolitan Museum of Art*. New York: Metropolitan Museum of Art, 1982.

Snorri Sturluson. *The Prose Edda*. Translated by Jesse L. Byock. New York: Penguin, 2005.

To Mom and Dad

ABOUT THIS BOOK

The illustrations for this book were done in pen and ink and watercolor on paper. This book was edited by Christy Ottaviano and designed by Véronique Lefèvre Sweet. The production was supervised by Lillian Sun, and the production editor was Marisa Finkelstein. The text was set in Atma Serif Book Roman, and the display type is Hillenberg Press Regular. The title type on the front cover and title page was created by the artist.